09/2015

I WON'T SHARE!

Copyright © 2005 by Hans Wilhelm, Inc.

All rights reserved. Published by Scholastic Inc.
SCHOLASTIC, CARTWHEEL BOOKS, NOODLES, and associated logos
are trademarks and/or registered trademarks of Scholastic Inc.
Lexile is a registered trademark of MetaMetrics, Inc.

Library of Congress Cataloging-in-Publication Data is available.

ISBN 978-0-439-77353-9

12   15/0

Printed in the U.S.A. 40 • This edition first printing, May 2010

I WON'T SHARE!

by Hans Wilhelm

SCHOLASTIC INC.

New York Toronto London Auckland
Sydney Mexico City New Delhi Hong Kong

This is my toy Squeaky.

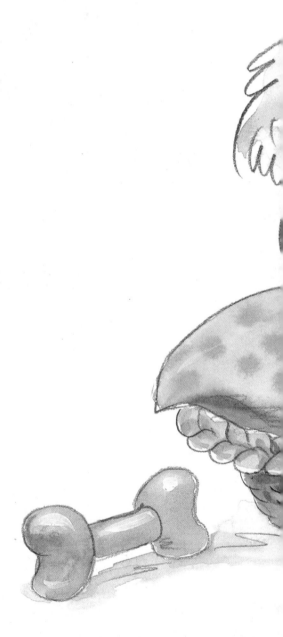

I love to play with Squeaky.

Let go!
It's *mine*!

Give me back my toy.

Wait!
That is *my* Squeaky.

Good!
He dropped it!

Grrrr...
I won't share!
Go away!

This is no fun.

I have an idea!

Hey!
Let's play catch!

Good catch, Buddy!

Get it, Scottie!

Now it's my turn.

I love this game.

Sharing is so much fun!